WITHDRAWN

Princess Smartypants Rules

ISBN 0-399-24349-6
1 3 5 7 9 10 8 6 4 2

Princess Smartypants Rules

Babette Cole

G. P. Putnam's Sons
New York

There was nothing Princess Smartypants loved doing more in
the whole Kingdom of Totaloonia,
than playing with
baby dragons.
They were such
clever little
creatures!

She thought it would be
so nice to have a baby
of her own.

She asked her parents if it was possible to have a baby without being married.

"Certainly NOT!" said her mother, the queen,
who was busy knitting sculptures for the Royal Art Exhibition.

"Bother!" said Princess Smartpants, who wasn't at all
keen on marrying a prince

"Enough of babies," said the Queen, "I'm putting you in charge of the banquet for the Grand Opening of my show. Make sure there's plenty of Royal Gravy – the guests will love it!"

Princess Smartypants hated cooking, so she phoned the royal grocer for a packet of ready-mix gravy.

But the line was a bit crackly . . .

"Yes, Your Totalooniness. One packet of ready-mix BABY on the way!" said the grocer.

Princess Smartypants was in a hurry. She didn't read the label, she just followed the instructions on the back.

1. Mix contents with half a pint of milk.

2. Stir violently over a red-hot heat.

3. Add plenty of pepper.

4. Leave to 'rise'
under a damp cloth.

The result was

INCREDIBLE!

Princess Smartypants
forgot about the gravy!

She was DELIGHTED
with her new baby . . .
although he did seem unusually
strong for his age.

The baby wrecked the exhibition. The royal
dignitaries all fled in terror – except for
her wicked uncle . . .

the evil
Count Rottenghut!

He snatched the baby . . .

and made off for Castle Creep, home of the despicable Prince Swashbuckle. The prince had never forgiven Smartypants for refusing to marry him and turning him into a toad!

With Rottenghut's help, he had been plotting to take over Totaloonia, ever since.

They thought the baby would be just
the secret weapon they needed!
"What a delightful child,"
drooled Prince Swashbuckle.
"You have done well,
my friend."

Princess Smartypants summoned her mighty dragons.
   "We must rescue my baby!" she commanded.
"He is dangerous in the wrong hands!"
   "I know what a responsibility babies are,"
said Amazonia Sizzleflame, "I've had three thousand!"

So, with Amazonia
in the lead, the squadron
of dragons zoomed off.

The dragons breathed their
fiery breath upon the castle
until it glowed red hot!
Its evil occupants ran out
and were captured
at once.

Smartypants and Amazonia
flew in through one window
and out of another,
grabbing the baby
on the way.

"There you are," said Smartypants to her parents,
"I have saved Totaloonia from deadly peril!"
    "Oh good," said her mother. "I'm glad
you're so brave, because you can rule . . .

while we take my exhibition on a world tour. And don't let that dreadful child destroy the kingdom while we're away!"

CRASH

Princess Smartypants soon found out that it was much easier to rule the kingdom than the baby . . .

Now that he knew his own strength, he was rapidly becoming the palace pest!

"Perhaps some people are just
not cut out to have babies,"
she sighed.

Then Princess Smartypants had a brilliant idea!
She asked Amazonia Sizzleflame if she
could have one of her eggs.
"Of course," said Amazonia. "I've got
far too many. Don't forget. You must
sleep on it for a week."

Poor Princess Smartypants didn't sleep a wink for a week!

But it was worth it!

The baby was very respectful of his new brothers, Pongo and Bongo. They kept him out of trouble and the castle was safe.

So when her parents rang to ask how the ruling was going,
Princess Smartypants could honestly say,
"I've got every little thing
under control!"